Bamboo and Me

Exploring Bamboo's Many Uses in Daily Life

This book is edited and designed by the Editorial Committee of *Cultural China* series.

Story by Xu Bin
Illustration by Yuan Yahuan
Translation by Yijin Wert
Design by Su Liangliang

Copy Editor: Anna Nguyen
Editor: Wu Yuezhou
Editorial Director: Zhang Yicong

Senior Consultants: Sun Yong, Wu Ying, Yang Xinci
Managing Director and Publisher: Wang Youbu

ISBN: 978-1-60220-454-6

Address any comments about *Bamboo and Me: Exploring Bamboo's Many Uses in Daily Life* to:

Better Link Press
99 Park Ave
New York, NY 10016
USA

or

Shanghai Press and Publishing Development Co., Ltd.
F 7 Donghu Road, Shanghai, China (200031)
Email: comments_betterlinkpress@hotmail.com

Printed in China by Shenzhen Donnelley Printing Co., Ltd.

1   3   5   7   9   10   8   6   4   2

Bamboo and Me

Exploring Bamboo's Many Uses in Daily Life

A Story Told in English and Chinese

By Xu Bin & Yuan Yahuan
Translated by Yijin Wert

Better Link Press

When spring came, I had a dream where a big red fish said to me, "Go to the bamboo forest to find a present."

春天到了，我做了一个梦，梦里一条红色的大鱼对我说："快到竹林里找礼物。"

The next day, I went up to the bamboo forest on the mountains with Dad, Mom, and my little brother.

第二天，我拉着爸爸妈妈和弟弟，上山到竹林去。

Dad and Mom began digging once we got deep into the forest. They turned out to be the bamboo shoots. My little brother and I loaded them up into a basket.

我们来到竹林深处，爸爸妈妈挖呀，挖呀。原来是竹笋呀。我和弟弟把它们码在背篓里。

We carried baskets full of bamboo shoots home, and
started to peel the hard outer skin off them.

背起满满的背篓，我们回家剥竹笋。

We used the skin of the bamboo shoots to
feed the old cows and the calves.

我们把笋壳喂给家里的老牛和小牛。

The bamboo shoots were boiled in a pot. After drained off the water, they were left out to become delicious dried bamboo shoots.

竹笋放锅里煮熟、沥干，美味的笋干做好了。

When summer came, I went to the bamboo forest looking for the present from my dream with Grandpa. We ended up cutting down a bunch of bamboo to take home.

夏天到了，我拉着爷爷到竹林里去找梦中的礼物。我们砍下一捆竹子搬回家。

Grandpa split the thick bamboo down the middle and cut them into sections.

爷爷把粗粗的竹子劈成两半，做成竹段。

My little brother and I helped Grandpa lay the bamboo sections down the hill.

我和弟弟帮着爷爷，把竹段一根一根顺着山坡连起来。

The spring water flowed down through the bamboo sections and ended up in our big water container.

Grandma used the water to clean vegetables. Mom used the water to wash clothes. My little brother and I had fun playing with the water.

清凉的溪水顺着竹段流啊流啊，一直流到家中的水缸里。奶奶洗菜，妈妈洗衣服，我和弟弟开开心心打水仗。

On still summer nights, the lighting bugs flew around us. Look! The bamboo was transformed into the fan in Grandpa's hand, bringing a gentle breeze.

宁静的夏夜，萤火虫一闪一闪地飞。瞧！竹子变成了爷爷手里的扇子，送来凉风习习。

The water was high in the little river. The bamboo was transformed into fishing poles, rakes and backpacks. We enjoyed fishing down there.

小河涨满了水，竹子变成了钓竿、钉耙和背篓。我和大伙儿下河捕鱼忙得欢。

At night, the bamboo was transformed into broom and dust pan. Using a flash light, it was even more fun to catch fish at the river beach.

晚上，竹子变成了扫帚和簸箕。我和小伙伴打着手电筒，在河滩抓鱼更有趣。

Look! The bamboo served as trays to lay out the leftover fish. The dried fish is a tasty snack.

瞧！竹子变成了匾。吃不完的鱼摊在竹匾上，美味鱼干就晒成了。

When autumn came, my little brother and I returned to the
bamboo forest to find the present from my dream.
We found Grandpa cutting the bamboo into sticks. "There is
no need to find a present. It's right by your side," he said.

秋天到了，我和弟弟去竹林里找梦中的礼物。
爷爷一边劈竹条，一边说，"不用找，礼物就在你们身边哦。"

Bend the bamboo stick
弯竹条

Assemble the frame
扎骨架

Paste the sail
糊纸

Dad shaped the light-weighted bamboo sticks into an
intricate big kite. We helped him paint the pattern on the sail.

爸爸用又薄又轻的竹条扎了一只大风筝。我们帮他画
上漂亮的图案。

The kite turned out to be the big red fish from my dream! The beautiful fish kite quickly flew up and soared into the sky.

啊，原来就是梦里的红色大鱼！漂亮的大鱼风筝飞呀飞呀，一直飞到高高的天上。

On Sundays, we played bamboo flutes as we walked to the market with Grandpa.

星期天，吹着竹笛，我们和爷爷去集市啦！

The market was bustling with people. We were selling our bamboo products, dried bamboo shoots and dried fish snacks. There we bought a lot of good food and presents to play with. It was fun!

集市上好热闹。我们卖竹器、卖竹笋、卖鱼干……再买很多好吃好玩的礼物，真开心啊！

Then the winter arrived. On Chinese New Year's eve, our family sat around the fire to have our special dinner. The pleasant aroma of the pork cooked with dried bamboo shoots carried through the air.

冬天来了，过年啦，我们围着火塘吃年夜饭，笋干和腊肉的香味弥漫在空气中。

But the bamboo forest was covered in snow. Would my present still be there?

可是竹林被厚厚的积雪覆盖着，那里还可以找到礼物么？

Oh, Grandpa had already prepared our presents long ago—the beautifully crafted bamboo pencil holders.

原来爷爷早就准备好了给我们的礼物——是竹子做成的漂亮笔筒。

We liked them so much that we took the pencil holders to bed with us and fell soundly asleep.

我们太喜欢爷爷做的笔筒，便握着它美美地睡着了。

Cultural Explanations
知 识 点

China was the first country in the world to grow bamboo and create products with it. Even today, bamboo can be found throughout the everyday lives of the Chinese people. It makes for an attractive decorative accent in many backyards. Bamboo can also be crafted into many products including baskets, trays, backpack, brooms, and flutes. Bamboo shoot is a popular food and could be added in a variety of dishes. The bamboo itself is even the panda's favorite food.

　　中国是世界上最早培育和利用竹子的国家。直至今天，竹子在中国人的日常生活中仍随处可见。竹子在院子里是可爱的装饰品，还可以做成篮子、盘子、背篓、扫帚和笛子等等。竹笋是受欢迎的美食，可以加到很多菜里。竹子还是大熊猫最喜欢的食物。